The Bee
Who Spoke

The wonderful world of Belle and the bee

To Ophelia and Bernard

The Bee Who Spoke © 2013 and 2014
Sunshine Partners Ltd and Mother London Ltd

Text by Al MacCuish
Illustrations by Rebecca Gibbon
Design by Ben McNaughton

First published in 2013 by Laboratoires M&L SA,
Z.I. St-Maurice, 04100-Manosque, France
www.melvita.com

This edition first published in 2014 in hardcover in the United States of
America by Thames & Hudson Inc., 500 Fifth Avenue,
New York, New York 10110

thamesandhudsonusa.com

Library of Congress Catalog Card Number 2014932796

ISBN 978-0-500-65027-1

Printed and bound in China by Toppan Leefung Printing Limited

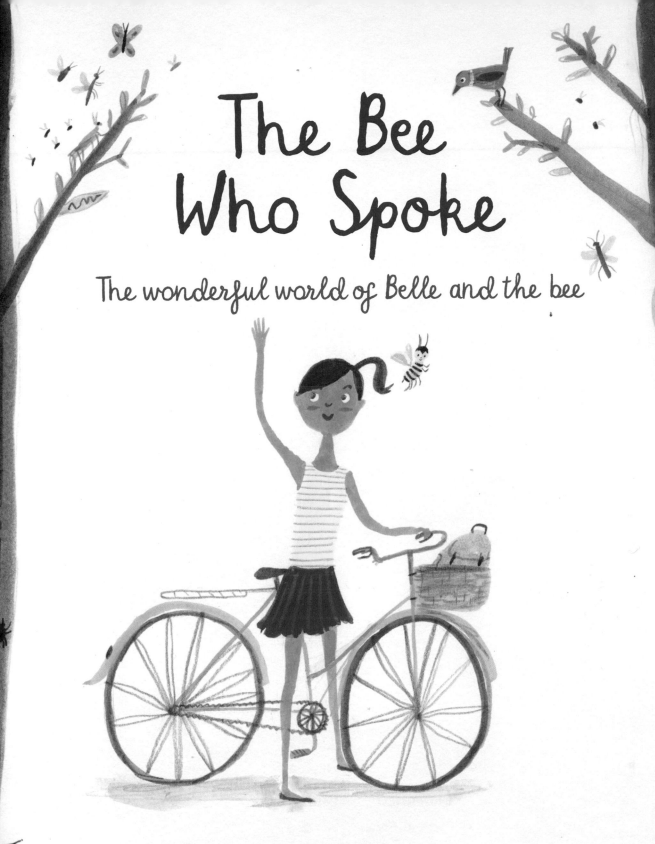

The Bee
Who Spoke

The wonderful world of Belle and the bee

Al MacCuish

Illustrations by Rebecca Gibbon

Thames & Hudson

Once upon a time in the great city of Paris, near Rue Saint-Rustique in the 18th arrondissement, there lived a girl named Belle.

Belle loved the city and the city loved her. She knew its alleys and avenues, its rhythms, noises, colors and people by heart.

She knew that Monsieur Talgard opened his bakery every morning at 7; Madame Babineau watered her sunflowers at 8, and the bells of the Sacré-Cœur marked 9 o'clock *a full minute* after all the other city bells.

But much as Belle loved the city and the city loved her, there was a small piece of her heart in another place altogether.

Every year around this time, as the days grew longer, the weather warmer and ice-cold lemonade became a priority, Belle and her parents would make a very special journey.

Belle's trip required careful preparation. For days beforehand, she packed and re-packed her bag with her most treasured possessions.

1 penknife, a gift from her father

5 pencils, each sharpened to a point

1 magnifying glass, polished to a shine

1 new camera, bought with savings

She added a croissant for emergencies and, last but not least, a brand new journal.

Belle

If you were to ask anyone in Montmartre about Belle, they would say: *"Ah! Belle sees it all!"*

So she did – and it was all recorded in her journals.

After a long journey spent singing songs and
playing memory games, they finally arrived
at her grandparents' house. Belle was bursting
with impatience.

Every year, Belle's grandfather would work all winter making a gift
for her. When she was very small, he gave her a hobby horse;

when she was a little older, a tree house;

then last year, a beautiful easel.

This year, her present was something *very special indeed*.

It was Belle's mother's bicycle from when she was a girl. Belle had gazed longingly at it a million times in the picture on her mother's dressing table. And now here it was, right before her, freshly painted and gleaming in the sun. She could hardly breathe for excitement.

Belle threw her bag in the basket, rang the bell twice, and headed off down the lane as fast as her feet would pedal.

"Don't get lost!" shouted
her father after her.

"Don't be late for tea!"
added her grandmother.

"Ride like the wind!" cried
her grandpa, laughing.

But Belle was already gone.

The first thing people from the city always notice when
they get to the countryside is the sky. It seems bigger,
bluer, more sky-like, stretching as far as the eye can see.

Belle saw clouds tumbling into one another; a bird hovering above a patchwork of fields; the tops of the trees swaying in the wind.

What she didn't see was the root of a great oak tree in her path.

There was a bump. Followed by a "*whoah!*" Followed by a clatter. Then an "*owww!*"

All the animals and insects fell silent. Even the breeze seemed to stop for a moment.

Belle looked down. Her skirt was covered in dust. She had a bruised knee. But worst of all, she had an uneasy feeling in her stomach. *She was lost.*

Belle didn't know the country and the country didn't know her.

"Hello?!" she called out, in her smallest voice.

"Hello!" came a friendly voice in reply.

But there was no one to be seen. Confused, Belle grabbed her scattered belongings. Then she noticed a little bee gently buzzing towards her. It inspected her croissant curiously.

Then it spotted Belle's journal on the ground.

"Belle," it remarked. "What a beautiful name."

Belle tried to speak but the words refused to come out. Finally three words did:

"*Bees can't talk*!" exclaimed Belle.

"Of course we can," said the bee. "You just have to know how to listen."

Belle had come in at the top of her class in biology but at no time had anyone ever mentioned that bees can talk.

The bee's voice was wise, thoughtful and kind. It made the bee seem much bigger than it was.

"I think I'm lost," said Belle. She was determined not to cry.

"Why, there is a map all around you," said the bee reassuringly.

But Belle could see only trees.

The bee buzzed a little closer and folded its arms, a bit like her biology teacher did when she was about to explain something new.

"Do you like adventures?" it asked.

"I live for them!" replied Belle, brightening.

"Then I'd like to take you on a little journey," said the bee.

The bee led Belle to a clearing full of flowers.

"Belle meet Arnica, Arnica meet Belle," said the bee.

She peered closer. The flower looked familiar.
Suddenly she remembered Madame Babineau's
window box:

"It looks like a tiny sunflower!" said Belle.

"They're cousins," said the bee, smiling.

The bee showed Belle how to take the petals, press them
between her hands, and then rub the oil on
her knee. At once the ache began to fade.

Belle's eyes widened in astonishment:

"That's..."

"...nature," finished the bee.

"Come. I have some more friends I'd like you to meet."

The bee knew everyone and everyone knew the bee.

"What a busy place!" said Belle, as they stopped
to let an army of ants pass on the forest floor.

"In nature, we all have a job to do," said the bee.

"What's yours?" asked Belle, as they arrived
at a particularly tall tree.

"Ah!" said the bee, puffing with pride.
"Nature gave us the most important job of all."

hup two, three, four,
hup two, three, four...

"We help everything grow," said the bee. "If there were no *bzzz* there would be no oranges for your orange juice, no strawberries for your jam – none of the delicious things."

Belle agreed that this would make for a very dull breakfast.

"We visit the plants and the bushes and the trees, and carry their precious pollen from one flower to another," said the bee.

"That's how nature makes new plants and flowers."

"Do you get any treats?" asked Belle, taking out her camera.

"Oh yes!" declared the bee. "We get nectar."

"To make honey!" cried Belle. Her biology teacher would have been proud.

They climbed high into a tree and Belle saw, for the very first time, a bee hive abuzz with busy activity.

"Everything seems ... just so," said Belle, marveling.

"Ah!" said the bee. "We have a saying for that."

"*La nature est bien faite*," said the bee, proudly.

Belle gave a quizzical look.

"A place and a purpose for everything – that's the beauty of nature," said the bee.

Belle gazed in wonder at the expanse of fields,
trees and sky before her.

"I can see grandpa's house!" she cried with delight.
"In fact, I can see *everything!*"

Then, remembering her journal: "I must write it
all down!"

And with that there followed the sound of a young
Parisian girl descending a tree at the speed of a girl
who could have spent her entire life climbing trees
in the country.

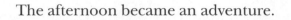

The afternoon became an adventure.

They skipped from place to place, the bee pointing,
Belle scribbling—when all of a sudden they heard *music*.

Belle got out her binoculars to investigate.

"My goodness!" she exclaimed.

They were being followed by a troupe of insects and animals
carrying what looked like little trombones (but were in fact
bluebells).

The birds broke into full song with their chests puffed out.

"I know this one!" said the bee, delighted. "Join in, Belle, if you can!"

And nature's song began:

You and me,
And the flowers
And the trees
And the birds in the bushes
And the seeds on the breeze,

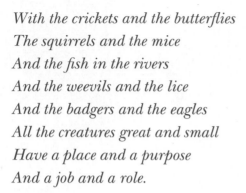

With the crickets and the butterflies
The squirrels and the mice
And the fish in the rivers
And the weevils and the lice
And the badgers and the eagles
All the creatures great and small
Have a place and a purpose
And a job and a role.

We are one and we are all
Or we're nothing much at all.

Thanks to the bee-ee
We live in harmon-ee.
Oi!
Thanks to the bee-ee
We live in harmon-ee!

A great cheer went up in the forest at the end and Belle
danced with delight.

With the greatest of patience, the bee continued to introduce
Belle to all the animals, including a large owl who talked in
his sleep. "Toowit toowoo, who are you?" he asked Belle blurrily.

Belle suddenly remembered her grandmother's words. It was
time to go home.

"May I come back tomorrow?" asked Belle.

The bee smiled. "You are always welcome here, dear Belle."

"Goodbye then!" cried Belle, as she turned her bike towards home.

And all at once, the insects and the birds and the animals stopped what they were doing and waved "goodbye" in a great chorus to their new friend.

Belle had the best time of her life that summer. Every day at sunrise, she would check her tires, sharpen her pencils, polish her magnifying glass and head off into the countryside, a new chapter in her journal just waiting to be written.

But before she knew it, the days started to get shorter and the morning air cooler. It was time to go home.

Belle found herself back in the city; its alleys and avenues, rhythms, noises and colors greeted her like old friends.

Belle now knew the country and the country knew her.

But the city wasn't jealous: for every tree in its gardens, every bird in its fountains and parks, and every flower in every window box was part of a grand scheme.

Belle understood that this scheme is simply life itself. And that we people are but a part of it.

"That's nature," she thought, dreamily. And somewhere, very far away, a little bee smiled and went back to its noble work.

Thank you to the bees, who help to give us all of these
delicious foods:

Almonds
Apples
Apricots
Avocados
Blackberries
Blueberries
Broccoli
Cauliflower
Cherries
Cranberries
Cucumbers
Honey
Kiwi
Lemons
Limes
Oranges
Peaches
Pears
Plums
Pumpkins
Raspberries
Strawberries
Tomatoes
Vanilla
Watermelons
Zucchini

Without them, it would be a very dull world indeed.